This book
belongs to

.......Madeline Hook........

Cuddle

The Magic Kitten

MAGICAL FRIENDS

Cuddle

The Magic Kitten

MAGICAL FRIENDS

by Hayley Daze

Willow
Tree

This edition published by Willow Tree Books, 2020
Willow Tree Books, Tide Mill Way, Woodbridge, Suffolk, IP12 1AP, UK
First published by Ladybird Books Ltd.

2 4 6 8 9 7 5 3

Series created by Working Partners Limited,
London, WC1X 9HH
Text © 2018 Working Partners
Cover illustration © 2018 Willow Tree Books
Interior illustrations © 2018 Willow Tree Books

Special thanks to Jane Clarke

ISBN: 978-1-78700-454-2
Printed and bound in Great Britain
by Bell and Bain Ltd, Glasgow

www.willowtreebooks.net

To Mom and Dad

Cuddle the kitten has black-and-white fur,
A cute crooked tail, and a very loud purr.
Her two best friends, Olivia and Grace,
Know Cuddle's world is a special place!

Just give her a cuddle, then everything spins;
A twitch of her whiskers, and magic begins!
So if you see a sunbeam, and hear Cuddle's bell,
You can join in the adventures as well!

Contents

Chapter One
The Magic of Friendship

As if by magic, a grinning face framed by springy brown curls popped up above Grace's backyard fence. Then, in a flash, it was gone. Grace rubbed her eyes. Maybe she was so lonely she was making up imaginary friends.

The curly head appeared again,

bobbing along the fence. Two hands gripped the top of the wooden slats and then the smiling face looked over.

"I'm Olivia," the curly-haired girl said. "My mom says you're our new neighbor."

"Hi," Grace replied. "I'm Grace." Her smile was as bright as her shiny yellow hair.

Olivia balanced on the toes of her purple ballet pumps. Grace's backyard had a sandbox, a bench, and an overgrown vegetable patch filled with juicy tomatoes and stringy beans. But Olivia was staring at a triangular-shaped pile of boxes in the middle of the lawn.

Cuddle
The Magic Kitten

"Nice pyramid," she said.

"Oh—thanks," Grace replied. "These are the removal boxes Mom and Dad have unpacked." She grabbed a box and placed it on the top of the pyramid. "I used to live on a farm. It's funny seeing so many tall buildings. I thought I'd make one myself!"

The sky above them darkened as gray clouds glided across the sun.

"Is it always cloudy in Catterton?" Grace asked.

Olivia nodded. "But don't worry, it doesn't mean we can't have fun. We can play dress-up indoors or chase rainbows in the backyard. The best thing about living here is there's always

someone to play with." She smiled.
"You just have to know where to look."

Olivia dropped down behind the
fence, out of sight. Grace jumped as
high as her sneakers would take her,
springing up and down, but it looked
like Olivia's backyard was empty.
She had vanished.

"Close your eyes," Olivia called.

Grace squeezed her eyes tightly
shut.

"Ta-dah!" Olivia said. Grace's eyes
snapped open. Olivia was standing
right in front of her.

"How did you do that?" Grace asked.
"It's like magic!"

Olivia's curls bounced as she shook

her head. "It's not magic," she said, taking Grace's hand. "But it can be our secret!"

Olivia showed her a section of the fence that was partly hidden by a rose bush. One of the panels of wood was hanging loose at the bottom. Olivia pulled it so it swung upward, making a gap just big enough to squeeze through.

"It's like a giant cat-flap," Grace said as she peeked into Olivia's backyard.

Olivia laughed. "You're right! Miss Nancy, the old lady who used to live in your house, had seven cats. We made the flap in the fence so I could come and play with them."

Cuddle
The Magic Kitten

Grace's mouth fell open. "Seven cats?"

"I wish I could have just one cat," Olivia sighed, "but my dad's allergic to them. He used to start sneezing if he even looked at one of Miss Nancy's cats."

"I can't have one either," Grace said. "I've got a new baby brother. Mom says I have to wait until he's older."

Olivia sat down on the bench, her shoulders slumped. The backyard felt empty without Miss Nancy's cats. "What should we do now?" she asked her new friend.

"I know! Let's see how far we can climb up that tree." Grace pointed to the apple tree at the foot of the backyard.

Olivia straightened her spotless denim skirt. "I'm not really dressed for climbing. But we could play movie star makeover. I'm going to be an actress one day, so I've got everything we need." She opened the sequinned purse which was slung across her shoulder and took out a hairbrush and some sparkly bobby pins.

A sudden burst of brightness made both girls shield their eyes. The gray clouds drifted apart and a sunbeam shone down onto Grace's backyard. It showered the cardboard pyramid with sparkling golden light.

Jingle jangle jingle.

Cuddle
The Magic Kitten

"Did you hear that?" Grace asked. "It sounded like a bell."

"Look!" Olivia shouted and pointed to Grace's cardboard tower.

Sitting at the top of the pyramid, eyes narrowed in the sunlight, was the cutest kitten either of the girls had ever seen.

Cuddle
The Magic Kitten

Chapter Two
The Jingle-Jangle Bell

The kitten's fur was white with one black ear and what looked like black socks on her two front paws. Her tail had a black tip and had a curly kink—like a fuzzy pipe-cleaner. Her pink tongue flicked in and out as she washed her paw. She turned her blue eyes toward the girls and gave a loud "Meow!"

Then, the tiny cat bounded down the pile of boxes and onto the grass. She was small enough to fit inside Olivia's bag. The girls knelt beside her, and the kitten stretched her head toward them.

"She wants to say hello," Grace said. She leaned down so she could bump heads with the kitten.

Olivia did the same and the kitten rubbed against her cheek.
"Your whiskers tickle," laughed Olivia.

Grace gave the kitten a stroke, from the tip of her pink nose to the curly kink in her tail. The kitten flopped onto her back, showing her white belly.

There was a *jingle jangle* as she rolled about, and the girls saw a tiny silver bell under her chin. It was attached to a sparkly pink collar.

"Miss Nancy's cats all had a name tag with her phone number on it," Olivia remembered. "Let's see who you belong to." She felt all around the kitten's collar, but there was nothing on it except the bell.

Grace tickled the kitten's belly. The little cat gave her fingers a lick, then stretched her paws up in the air. "Look, she wants a cuddle," Grace said.

Olivia rubbed the velvety tip of the kitten's nose.

"Cuddle," she said thoughtfully. "You

know, she likes being stroked and tickled. Cuddle is the perfect name for her."

The kitten gave a "Meow!" as if she agreed.

Grace laughed. "Cuddle it is."

With a flick of her tail, Cuddle rolled onto her belly. She crouched low to the ground, looking up at the girls.

"What is it, Cuddle?" Olivia asked. "Do you want to play?"

Cuddle bounded toward the cardboard pyramid. She scampered round it, her bell jingling, then hopped onto one of the boxes. The pyramid wobbled as she jumped from box to box, right to the top.

"Oh no," said Grace. "It's going to fall."

Just as the pyramid tumbled to the ground, Cuddle sprang through the air and landed safely in Olivia's arms.

"You crazy kitten," Olivia said, cradling her. Grace stroked Cuddle's silky black ears.

Purrrrrrrrr, went Cuddle.

Olivia wriggled. She felt ticklish all over. "Do you feel...tingly?" she asked Grace.

Grace nodded.

The girls started to giggle. Cuddle purred even louder and the tickling sensation grew stronger and stronger.

The backyard became a blur of greens and browns. The girls were laughing so much that both of them closed their eyes, and the world disappeared around them...

***

Chapter Three
Sandy Surprise

Grace wondered if she was in bed.
Maybe she was dreaming about a new
friend and a cute kitten. She was lying
down, covered in something warm.
It didn't feel like her soft blanket,
though—it was grainy, and she could
move her fingers through it. She opened

her eyes and gasped. "Sand!"

The mound of sand next to her stirred and Olivia sat up, shaking the grains from her curls.

"This is one of your magic tricks, isn't it—like you did with the fence?" Grace asked, feeling silly. "You've made us appear in the sandbox."

But Olivia's eyes were wide with astonishment. "Grace," she said slowly. "We're not in your backyard anymore."

Instead of wooden fences and big brick buildings, Olivia and Grace were surrounded by sand—lots and lots of sand—dotted with palm trees. The sky was deep blue and the air shimmered with heat. Cuddle was a few paces

away, shaking sand from her black-and-
white fur. She meowed as if to say
hello as the girls ran over to her.

"Was it you, Cuddle? Did you bring us here?" Grace asked. She remembered the tickling sensation and the kitten's loud purr before she closed her eyes.

Cuddle rubbed against Grace's leg. She flicked her crooked tail and leaped into Grace's arms. Her eyes narrowed as if she knew a secret.

"It's like she's saying yes," Olivia said, scratching Cuddle's chin.

"A magic kitten," Grace exclaimed. "That's amazing!"

Olivia pointed into the distance. "And so is that."

Grace turned to look. Towering in front of them was a gigantic pyramid. Its smooth sides were made from white stone and gleamed in the sunlight. Crouched beside it was an enormous statue with a human head and a lion's body, its front paws stretched out.

Grace couldn't believe her eyes. "A real pyramid," she said. "And what kind of creature is that statue?"

"A sphinx," Olivia said. "I saw it in a film once."

"Wow! We're in Egypt." Grace gave Cuddle an excited squeeze. "Let's go and look at the old pyramid. Maybe we'll find some mummies!"

"Grace," Olivia said, her eyes bright. "Does that pyramid look old to you?"

Grace tilted her head and stared at its polished white surface. The profile of the sphinx next to it was crisp and without a single chip. She gasped. "It's brand new. But that means..."

"...we're in Ancient Egypt!" Olivia

finished.

Cuddle
jumped from
Grace's arms.
Her crooked
tail bounced
and her bell jingled as
she scrambled up a sand
dune and skidded down the other side.

"Cuddle, come back!" Grace called.

The girls raced after her. The kitten
was running towards a group of purple-
and-blue tents under a clump of palm
trees. A young girl about their age
emerged from one of the tents. She was
wearing a white linen dress with a wide
gold necklace. Her hair was long and

black and on her wrist was a bracelet
shaped like a snake.

She gave a cry as Cuddle jumped
into her arms.

"Is this your kitten?" she asked the girls with a smile. "She's beautiful."

"Her name's Cuddle," Olivia said. "I'm Olivia, and this is Grace."

The girl handed Cuddle to Grace. "I am Beset," she said. She looked at Olivia's denim skirt and Grace's cargo pants. "Do you come from a land far away?"

Grace and Olivia glanced at each other. "That's one way of putting it," Grace replied.

"Welcome, Grace and Olivia," Beset said. "You must be here for the celebration." A frown spread over her face. "But I am afraid it may already be ruined."

"Oh, no!" Olivia exclaimed.

"The guest of honor—she is missing," Beset explained.

"That's terrible. Maybe we can help you find her." Grace scanned the landscape. "She should be easy to spot in all this sand."

"What does she look like?" Olivia asked.

"She is as black as night and has a fine silky coat," Beset said.

Olivia pictured a beautiful woman in one of those expensive coats she'd seen movie stars wear. "It seems too hot for a coat," she said.

"Cleo is like your kitten—she does not mind the heat," Beset said, giving

Cuddle a scratch behind the ear. Cuddle purred and wriggled happily in Grace's arms.

"The guest of honor is a cat?" Grace said in surprise.

Beset nodded. "Cleo is the pharaoh's kitten. He is hosting a banquet in her honor."

"Who is the pharaoh?" Olivia asked.

"The pharaoh is the king of all of Egypt," Beset replied. She looked even more worried. "If I do not find Cleo soon, the pharaoh will be sad, and I will be in big trouble."

Chapter Four
Cuddle Leads the Way

"Don't worry, Beset," Grace said. "We'll help you find Cleo."

"Thank you!" Beset said.

"Why are you having a party for a cat?" Olivia asked, trying not to giggle.

"Cats are very important to us," Beset said. "We even have a special goddess to protect them."

Cuddle hopped down onto the sand. "Meow!" The kitten rubbed against Beset's sandals, then darted off toward the pyramid.

"Cuddle!" Grace called. "Come back!" The kitten stopped running. But then she meowed at the girls and ran off again. The pink pads on her paws flashed as she bounded across the sand.

"I think she wants us to follow her," Olivia said.

The three girls chased after the little kitten, and they soon reached the pyramid. Palm trees were planted at each of the pyramid's four corners, their green leaves dancing in the

Cuddle
The Magic Kitten

sunshine. Cuddle's bell jingled as she dashed around one of the pyramid's corners. The girls followed—but the kitten had disappeared.

"Oh my," Beset said. "Now we will have to find two missing kittens."

Grace crouched down in the sand. "Look at this." Olivia and Beset peered over her shoulder at two sets of tiny paw prints.

"They must belong to Cuddle and Cleo. We can follow them to see where they've got to."

The paw prints wound through the sand and stopped at a white stone in the base of the pyramid. Pictures were engraved in the stone.

"I like that one," Grace said, pointing to a bird with long legs.

"They're a special kind of picture," Beset explained. "They tell a story. We call them hieroglyphs."

Olivia gave a shout of surprise. "Hey, look at this hieroglyph."

It was a cat with a curly kink in its tail.

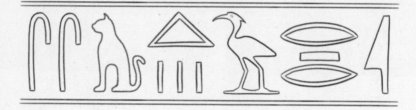

"It looks just like Cuddle," Grace said.

Beset ran her fingers over the cat hieroglyph. The stone wobbled slightly. "Did you see that?" she said. "Maybe this is a secret way into the pyramid."

The three girls placed their hands on the cat hieroglyph and pushed.

With a rumble, the stone slid inside the pyramid.

Grace gasped. "It's a secret passageway!"

Chapter Five
The Twisty-Turny Maze

Grace crawled through the dusty
passageway on her hands and knees.
At the end was a dark hole in the floor.
She peered down—it was a narrow
shaft. Her heart thumped as she swung
her legs over the edge of the hole and
let herself fall. She landed in a long,

wide corridor with flaming torches
flickering on the walls. The air was hot
and sticky.

Beset climbed after her, then Olivia.

"Yuck," Olivia muttered, pausing to
brush the thick dust from her skirt.

Beset walked ahead, her snake bracelet glinting in the torchlight. "There are many, many corridors," she said. "Cuddle and Cleo could be anywhere." She shook her head. "We will never find them in time.

The pharaoh will be very unhappy if Cleo does not come to her own celebration."

"Don't worry. I'm sure we can find them in time," Grace said, as she and Olivia hurried after Beset.

Passages led off in all directions, their entrances casting shadows like smudges on the smooth yellow floor.

Olivia twisted one of her curls around her finger. It was damp from the warm air. "How do we decide where to look first?"

Beset frowned. "The men who build the pyramids hide riddles and games inside them—like the secret passageway. Maybe we need to use a riddle to find the way."

Grace began to chant, moving her finger from one corridor to the next with each word. "Eeny, teeny, tiny cat, can you tell me where she's at? Strokes and snuggles, she loves all that, eeny, teeny, tiny cat." Grace finished the rhyme toward a corridor on the right. "Let's try that way."

The girls walked down the corridor, calling the two kittens' names. It was lined with tall ceramic jars. The lid of each jar was shaped like a bird's head with jeweled eyes that twinkled as the girls passed. The corridor twisted around a corner—and finished at a blank wall.

"It's a dead end," groaned Grace.

Disappointed, they wound their way back—and saw a little kitten curled up on the floor on the spot where they had started.

"Cuddle!" Olivia cried.

Cuddle rolled onto her back and stretched her paws toward the girls. Grace tickled her belly and Cuddle purred loudly.

"We've found one kitten," Beset said. "But now we must find Cleo."

Grace said her rhyme again, and this time they went down a corridor on the left. Cuddle sat on Olivia's shoulder, her head poking through Olivia's curls.

Cuddle

The Magic Kitten

The corridor swung left, then right, then left again, winding backward and forward until the girls had no idea which direction they had come from. They stopped by a tall statue of a bird with a hooked beak.

"This place is a maze," Grace said.

"Meow."

"That's not a real bird, Cuddle!" Olivia said. "It's just—"

Grace put her finger to her lips.

"Meow."

"That's not Cuddle meowing," Grace said. "It's coming from far away."

Beset clapped her hands in delight. "It must be Cleo!"

Chapter Six
All in the Dark

Cuddle leaped from Olivia's shoulder in a flurry of black-and-white fur. Her bell jingled as she scurried along the corridor, her crooked tail twitching behind her.

"Maybe she knows where Cleo is," Olivia said. She grabbed Grace and

Beset's hands and they raced after
Cuddle. The kitten led them down
winding corridors and into a great
chamber.

"Wow!" Grace said.

The ceiling above them was taller
than her new house. Torches glowed in
the branches of palm trees made
of gold.

Cuddle
The Magic Kitten

Whoosh!

A gust of warm wind swept through
the chamber. It blew out the torches,
leaving them in complete darkness.
The girls cried out in surprise. Grace
huddled next to Olivia. "I don't like the
dark much," she whispered. Her hands
shaking, Grace reached into the pockets
of her cargo pants. She felt rubber
bands, candy wrappers and a stick of
chewing gum, before pulling out the
small blue flashlight she always carried.
Flicking it on, she circled the narrow
beam of light around the room.

"I have never seen such a torch
before," Beset said. "Is it magical?"

"It's like the ones on the walls,

but you can turn it on and off," Grace
explained.

Cuddle's bell jingled and Grace trained the beam on her as she disappeared into the darkness. The girls followed, Grace lighting their way as best she could.

Cuddle stopped by a stone door. Grace moved the small flashlight over it. The door was covered in carvings of cats of all shapes and sizes: playing with string, chasing their tails, and rolling around.

"I see what you mean, Beset," Olivia said. "Egyptians really do love cats!"

Cuddle meowed and scrabbled against the door with her paws.

"Is Cleo in there?" Beset asked.

"Only one way to find out,"

Cuddle
The Magic Kitten

Grace replied.

The girls pushed against the door. It was stiff, and made a grinding noise as it opened a little.

Grace poked her head through the gap. She flashed the flashlight around, glimpsing enormous legs, jagged teeth—and a pair of massive eyes staring straight at her. "It's a monster!"

Cuddle
The Magic Kitten

Chapter Seven
Cat Chase

Beset took the flashlight from Grace, her shaking hands making the beam of light wobble. She slowly peeked around the door—and started to laugh.

"It is just a statue," she said.

Grace and Olivia followed her into the room. Beset trained the light on a wooden statue, twice as tall as a man. It had a human body and a head like a dog's. Its eyes were made from glittering emeralds.

"What kind of creature is it?" Grace asked.

"That is not a creature," Beset said. "It is Anubis—one of our gods. He looks after people when they die."

Jingle jangle jingle.

Cuddle came in behind them. Beset shone the light on the little kitten and she wiggled her whiskers. The girls gasped as a torch on the wall burst into flame, then another, and another, until the room was bathed in light.

"Did Cuddle do that?" Beset asked, her eyes wide.

Grace tickled the kitten's ears. "I wouldn't be surprised. She brought us here, after all."

"Cuddle," Olivia said, giving the kitten a kiss on the head, "you are cute and clever!"

The room was filled with glittering treasures. Opposite the statue of Anubis was a golden sphinx—like the one they had seen outside only much smaller. Silver plates and jugs stood piled

by thick cushions. Olivia knelt by a
turquoise chest brimming over with
necklaces, bracelets, and jewels.

Grace ran her hand over the smooth
head of a cat carved from green stone.
There were cat statues sitting neatly in
lines, some crouched on their haunches,
one washing its fur with a flickering

pink tongue...hold on, that statue was moving!

"Beset—I think I've found Cleo," Grace said.

Beset gave a cry of delight. But Cleo darted away, a streak of short black fur and bright blue eyes.

Cuddle sprang onto the head of the golden sphinx. "Meow!"

"Meow!" Cleo replied. She bounded

out from behind Anubis, pranced up the sphinx's back, and sat next to Cuddle. Her black fur was covered in dust.

"I think Cleo would rather play with Cuddle than go to the celebration," Grace said.

Beset sat down with a sigh. "You are correct. Cleo has many celebrations to attend. However, I do not think she enjoys them. Being the pharaoh's kitten does not leave much time for playing."

Olivia tugged on one of her curls, her lips pursed together thoughtfully. "Maybe we could make it more fun for her."

"That would be lovely," Beset said. "But how?"

"We can make her a new toy," Grace said and opened the pockets on her cargo pants, tipping shiny foil, a popsicle stick, a seashell, twine, and a drinking straw onto the floor. Olivia emptied lip balm, a hairbrush, and sparkly bobby pins from her bag.

Cuddle jumped down from the sphinx and bounded over. Cleo trotted to sit beside her, sniffing the heap of objects.

Beset caught Cleo at last, and nuzzled the top of her furry head. "You are very messy," she said. "You cannot go to the celebration like this."

Olivia picked up her hairbrush from the pile. "No problem. I'll make her look fit for a pharaoh. It's kitten makeover time!"

Beset put Cleo in Olivia's lap, and Olivia brushed the dust off her fur. Cuddle gave her a lick too, and soon Cleo's coat was gleaming.

"She looks glorious," Beset said reaching into the pocket of her gown and drawing out a collar. It was studded with glittering red jewels, each shaped like a tiny paw print. "This is Cleo's special celebration collar," she said, slipping it over the kitten's head.

"It's beautiful," Olivia said.

"Here," called Grace. She was holding the popsicle stick. The twine was tied to the top, and knotted along its length were all the other objects.

Right at the end were Olivia's sparkly bobby pins.

Grace shook the stick and the

objects jiggled.

"Meow!" Cleo pounced on the twine, making the girls laugh.

"She can play with her new toy during the celebration," Olivia said. "That's great, Grace."

"Thank you, Olivia and Grace," Beset said, but she still looked worried. "But how will we make it to the celebration in time if we can't find our way back out of the pyramid?"

Cuddle
The Magic Kitten

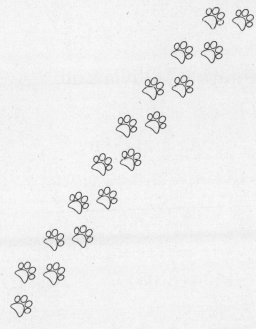

Chapter Eight
Join the Parade

Olivia and Grace looked at each other.

"Cuddle brought us here..." Olivia began.

"...and she'll show us the way out," Grace said.

The black-and-white kitten raced back through the pyramid. Cleo followed her, the toy in her mouth, with the girls behind. As Cuddle flashed past, each of the torches on the walls magically sprang into flame, lighting their way through the darkness.

They crawled out through the secret

passageway, tumbling over each other onto the sand.

The air rang with cheering and clapping that seemed to be coming from the other side of the pyramid.

"What's happening?" Grace

wondered, climbing to her feet.

"The celebration is about to start," Beset said. "We must hurry! Follow me!"

Grace carried Cuddle and Olivia carried Cleo, while Beset led them around the pyramid.

A parade of people were dancing across the sand, their white robes and jeweled necklaces shimmering in the sun. They were heading toward a large group of purple-and-blue tents.

The girls hurried to the front of the parade. Four attendants were carrying an enormous cushion, as blue as Cleo's eyes. Beset placed Cleo in the middle of it, and the crowd cheered. The little black kitten rolled around, batting the toy with her paws.

Olivia and Grace joined the dancing crowd, laughing as they took it in turns to twirl Cuddle around.

Beset and Cleo led the parade into the largest tent. The tent was filled with tables laden with fruit and delicious pastries, and in the center was a beautiful golden throne. A man was sitting in it, wearing a tall red-and-white crown.

"He must be the pharaoh," whispered Grace, hugging Cuddle to her.

Beset placed Cleo at the pharaoh's feet. The kitten rubbed against his jeweled sandals, and Beset bowed low

to the ground. Grace and Olivia did the
same, but Cuddle sprang from Grace's

arms. She jumped onto the arm of the golden throne and seemed to bow to the pharaoh.

Olivia held her breath. Would the pharaoh be cross?

But he smiled and stroked Cuddle, all the way from her nose to the curly tip of her tail. "Cats are very special," he said. "Some might say magical. Thank you for returning Cleo to me."

When the girls bowed again, Cuddle leaped down from the throne, pushing through the crowd.

"Goodbye, Pharaoh! Goodbye, Beset!" the girls called. They followed Cuddle out of the tent and back into the heat of the desert.

Olivia gazed around at the vast
sandy landscape. She suddenly missed
Catterton's neat rows of houses and

leafy backyards filled with flowers.
"We found Cleo, but now we're the
ones who are lost," she said. "How will

we ever find our way home?"

The little kitten rubbed against the girls' legs, weaving around their feet in looping figures of eight.

Her purr grew louder, and the sand, the pyramid, the sphinx, and the parade became a whirl of color.

"Cuddle's taking us home," Olivia whispered.

The girls held hands tightly and closed their eyes as Ancient Egypt melted away...

***

When Olivia opened her eyes, they were in Grace's backyard. The apple tree, the cardboard boxes, the sandbox—everything seemed exactly the same.

Grace scratched her head. "What just happened? Did Cuddle really take us to Ancient Egypt?"

"I think so," Olivia said, "but now I can't see her anywhere."

Jingle jangle jingle.

The girls spun around. Cuddle was walking along the top of the fence that separated their two backyards. She flicked her crooked tail and lifted her little black paw in what looked like a wave. Then, in a haze of sparkles, she disappeared.

"Goodbye, Cuddle," Grace said. "Do you think we'll see her again?"

"I hope so," Olivia replied with a smile. "Maybe she'll take us on another adventure."

"You know," Grace said, her eyes shining, "I think I'm going to love living here."

Cuddle
The Magic Kitten

Can't wait to find out
what Cuddle will do next?
Then read on! Here is the first
chapter from Cuddle's second
adventure, Superstar Dreams...

Cuddle

The Magic Kitten

SUPERSTAR DREAMS

A breeze rippled through the cherry tree, making its pink blossom dance. Grace's cargo pants and T-shirt were scattered with sweet-smelling petals.

"It's like being in a snowstorm of petals," she called down to Olivia. "Climb up and see."

Cuddle
The Magic Kitten

"I've never climbed a tree before," Olivia said, twirling one of her curls around and around a finger.

The girls were in Olivia's backyard. Grace was sitting in the cherry tree,

while Olivia stood beside the trunk.

From her perch, Grace could see her own backyard next door. The roofs of the houses that lined their street were still damp from a rain shower. The sky over Catterton was dark gray.

"Let's see if you can get up here before it rains again," Grace said. "I'll help you."

"All right," Olivia said. "Here goes." Stretching up onto the tips of her shoes, she grabbed the lowest branch.

"That's it," Grace said. "Now wrap your legs around the trunk and hold the next branch."

Olivia could see Grace's smiling face through the leaves, framed by her blonde hair. She stretched up for the branch, but her fingers slid over a patch of moss. With a shriek, she tumbled to the ground.

Grace scrambled down after her. "Are you ok?"

Olivia was lying on the ground, her black curls fanned out like a halo. "I'm fine," she said, smiling. "Now do you believe I can't climb trees?"

Grace pulled Olivia to her feet. "You just need to practice. Then you'll be able to climb like a cat!"

Just then, a sunbeam pushed its way through the clouds, scattering golden rays.

Olivia clapped her hands. "Oh!

Do you think Cuddle's on her way?"

Cuddle was a cute kitten who had appeared in a beam of sunlight and taken the girls on a magical adventure.

Jingle jangle jingle.

"That's Cuddle's bell!" Grace cried.

The sunbeam shone on Olivia's bike, which was propped up against the back of the house. A pink basket was fixed to the handlebars. It wiggled and jiggled, and Cuddle's cute little face poked out. Her blue eyes sparkled in the sun.

"Hello, Cuddle!" both girls cried.

Olivia grinned. "The sunbeam looks like a spotlight. Cuddle's a movie star."

The kitten's bell jingled as she

sprang onto the edge of the bike's basket. With a swish of her tail, she leaped into Grace's arms and greeted her friends with a happy "Meow!"

Grace hugged the kitten tightly. "You certainly live up to your name, don't you, Cuddle?" she said.

Purrrrrrrr, went Cuddle. She sounded like a tiny rumble of thunder.

The girls' skin tingled as if Cuddle's whiskers were tickling them. Cuddle's purr grew louder and louder, and the girls started to giggle. They leaned into each other, the little kitten cradled between them.

Now they knew what would happen next—kitten magic! They each shut their eyes and the backyard and the cherry tree faded away...

***

Grace's eyes fluttered open. She was
lying on a hard surface in the pitch
dark. She closed her eyes and tried
opening them again, but it was no good.
She couldn't see a thing.

"Olivia?" Grace asked. She could feel
her heart thumping.

"I'm here," said Olivia. The two girls
were lying side by side.

Olivia knew that Grace was afraid
of the dark, and squeezed her friend's
hand. *"Where are we?"* she wondered.